I AM

DIFFERENT

I AM DIFFERENT

By Paula Range

Illustrated by Paula Range

Cover picture credit to:

Canva.com

This book is dedicated to a person who is a true treasure in my heart. You are an amazing person.

Some do not see what I see. They do not see the beauty in being different than them. If others could see that being different is not a bad thing, but a good thing, then they would see you for who you really are. An amazing, talented, hardworking young man. A young man who will stand by their loved one's side and will love and treat others like they are a treasure.

Please know that you are deeply loved, and some of us see the amazing man you are becoming. You are not invisible. We see you for who you truly are. And guess what? It's a good thing. *A very good thing indeed.*

A big *THANK YOU* to Makayla and Krista for helping me get this book out with the holidays quickly approaching.

PROLOGUE

Visions. What in the world was happening to me? Falling out of a treehouse, I hit my head on a rock. Sadly, it had been on a Friday after school with my "friends", so I had all weekend to rest. So, what did that mean? It meant that I didn't get to skip any school. Bummer.

Ever since my fall, I have been seeing visions of people's lives. Not just anyone, but people who'd been bullied by me or others. Am I a bully? Well, hopefully not anymore. But *was* I a bully? To answer truthfully, YES, I WAS A BULLY.

When I started school, my friends were the cool kids. But as the visions began, I slowly saw who I was and who the other kids I had been hurting were. My choice of friends slowly changed. I say "choice" of friends because I realized I had a choice. I could step away from bullying others or continue the road I was on.

I chose to step away. May I say, that was the best choice I had ever made. I did not say the easiest, but the best for me.

So, come join me, read on and see where my next visions will take me.

CHAPTER 1

Moving. I can't believe my parents were moving us across town. Don't get me wrong, a new house sounds *awesome,* but not when it involves riding the school bus every single day.

Being in the eighth grade, I have gone my whole life without having to ride the bus. My sixth-grade sister, Grace, and I lived close enough that we either walked to the middle school, or my parents would drive us. But since my dad sprung the news that we were moving in just a couple of weeks, it sent me into a full-fledged panic.

Now I found myself standing in the driveway looking at my new house. As I looked around I noticed it was a lot windier out at this house because there were no trees. I shivered wearing only my fall jacket. The end of November was so cold in Michigan. Shoot! I should have grabbed my hat and gloves. I wanted to get inside where it was warm, but my sister Grace was chatting away with my parents about the houses next door.

Then my dad said to my sister and me, "Hey girls, see that house right next door? That's the one I was talking about. I work with the dad, and he said they have a boy Cat's age."

Grace just wiggled her eyebrows at me and said, "Cat has a boyfriend!"

Rolling my eyes, I said, "Good grief, get real."

"Oh, come on Cat, dream a little. You never know! He may be your prince charming!" Bursting out laughing, Grace started to walk towards our front door. Just then I heard someone yell out to my dad.

"Oh, hi, Bill!" my dad hollered back and waved.

I turned and watched as a family stepped out of the exact house my dad had just been pointing at. A little redheaded girl with pigtails stood right next to her mom, clinging to her leg. Next out of the house came a boy who looked around my age. With brown hair a little longer than most boys in eighth grade, he stood tall and just stared at us. Turning, I continued to walk toward our new house when my dad motioned us to follow him.

"Come on kids, let me introduce you all."

I followed my family as they walked over to the neighbor's house.

"Girls, this is the man from work I was telling you about."

We started to make introductions, with everyone either shaking hands, or giving a shy smile. They introduced the boy as Jonah.

I quickly glanced over at him, and to my surprise he was looking straight at me. Before I could look away, our eyes connected. I faintly heard my dad exclaim, "Kids, meet your new neighbors," just as I started to see stars...

CHAPTER 2

Jonah was at school taking a test. His hands were sweating. Other kids were starting to hand in their tests. He looked down at his paper and tried to read the first question.

Next, someone started to walk up and hand in their test, while walking by and bumping into Jonah's arm a little too hard, causing Jonah's test to fall to the floor.

"Oops, sorry, why don't I get that for you." The boy said with a mean grin on his face.

"No, I've got it," Jonah answered, trying to reach his paper first.

But the boy got to it before Jonah could. Looking at the blank paper, he handed it back and laughed. "What's wrong, dummy? Oh, wait, I know." He leaned in towards Jonah and said, "You can't read. How did you get all the way to eighth grade without reading?"

"Knock it off," Jonah huffed, trying to look like he was busy with his test.

"Yeah, just keep acting like you know what the paper says. It doesn't fool us." The boy motioned around the room. "We all know you're stupid."

He gave one more dirty look towards Jonah and walked to the front of the room to hand in his test.

Jonah watched as the boy handed it to the teacher. Soon the whole class had their test turned in, and everyone was starting to talk. As the room grew louder and louder, Jonah started to panic. Class was almost over, and he hadn't gotten one answer down. Quickly, he just colored in a circle bubble for each question.

As the bell rang to show class was over, Jonah quickly walked up to the front of the room and handed in his test.

"How did it go, Jonah?" his teacher asked.

"Fine." He mumbled as he walked out of class.

As he opened his locker, he heard the same boy walk by talking to his friends, "Yeah, he didn't have one answer done yet on his test. I can't believe he can't read!"

"I know," Jonah heard another kid say, "he's so dumb!"

And as they walked off, Jonah couldn't tell anymore what they were saying. He slumped his shoulders, because he knew the words spoken were not a lie; he couldn't read, and he was stupid.

"Cat!" My dad called out. "I said, meet your new neighbors."

I snapped out of my vision.

"Um, hi." I squeaked out.

"Hi, this is my wife, Heather, our son, Jonah, and our daughter, River."

I looked and saw the little girl, who I was guessing was maybe around six or seven years old, hiding behind her mom's body, just peeking her head out. Their son Jonah was shaking my dad's hand.

"Well, it was nice to finally meet your family, Bill. We're just going to show our kids our new house. We'll see you around."

As we turned and walked off, Grace grabbed my arm and tucked hers into mine and whispered, "Wow, Cat, that boy's so cute!"

"But, don't you remember what you said? He's *my* prince charming." Teasing my sister, I raised my eyebrows.

"Yeah, about that. Forget what I said. He's really not your type."

"Oh, so he's not my type, but you think he's yours?"

With a dreamy-eyed look, my sister answered, "He's exactly my type." Laying a hand against her heart, she added, "He's perfect, absolutely perfect."

CHAPTER 3

As I got ready for school the next day, I couldn't stop thinking about the vision I had of the new kid next door. How could someone be in eighth grade and not be able to read? It made no sense to me.

Ever since I hit my head on a rock, I'd been seeing visions of people's lives who had been bullied. At first it was kinda scary, but now I realize how words can really crush a person. Now I try to help others instead of hurting them.

Since I'm great at English, maybe I could teach Jonah how to read. Yes, that is a great idea. I'd help him read, and Grace would bake brownies and cookies for him.

Last night Grace had come into my room all excited and said she was going to bake for him, because my mom had always told us that the way to a man's heart is through his stomach. I think my mom said that because my dad liked to eat so much. I don't think she was trying to get her eleven-year old daughter to bake for a cute neighbor boy.

Chuckling to myself, I finished up in the bathroom and went down to join everyone for breakfast.

Today was going to be Jonah's first day of school, so I was planning on introducing him to all my friends. Becky, Tyler, and Dallas would probably really like him. I only had one fear. If he couldn't read very well, then there were a few people I would have to keep him away from. I was determined that I wasn't going to let Holly, Amy, Tiffany, or Trent tease him. I was going to protect him from being bullied at our school.

As I grabbed my winter coat and slipped on my boots, only one thought remained.

How does a person protect someone from ever being bullied?

As my school day began, I thought it was going pretty good. For some reason Holly and Trent weren't in first hour today, so we were able to avoid them so far. I was able to introduce

Jonah to my friends, and so far, everyone liked him, *especially the girls.*

Finally, sixth hour came. He was in my class, which was fine, except so were Holly and Trent. My teacher asked everyone to grab a partner and read a chapter in our history books. I was just about to walk over and ask Jonah if he wanted to be my partner, when Holly beat me to it.

I watched as she batted her long eyelashes at him and asked in a sweet voice, "Hey Jonah, since you're new, do you want to be my partner? I can show you what she wants us to read."

I looked over and saw that Trent was mad. I think he was going to ask Holly to be his partner.

"Uh, sure," Jonah replied.

I groaned. She was the one I was trying to protect him from. Now what? Well, I didn't have to wait long. Within the first five minutes I heard Holly yell out, "What's wrong with you? I said it's your turn to read the next paragraph."

"I was just wondering if you could read the next one too."

Holly looked at him like he was crazy. "But I just read the first *three* chapters already!" She then agreed, "Fine, I'll do the next one, but you *have* to read after that."

I couldn't concentrate on my reading, so I found myself just watching to see what would happen next.

Holly finished up, and now it was Jonah's turn. I could actually see sweat dripping down his forehead. He didn't look around at anyone, just at his book. With his face beet-red he started, "In 1864 the... p..p...olice."

"No, you idiot! What's wrong with you? It says 'people', not 'police'."

People all around me started to snicker.

Jonah jumped up out of his chair and rushed out of the room.

"Holly! What did you do?" My teacher demanded.

"Me? Nothing!" Holly looked around at all of us with a snicker. "But the new kid can't read. Can you believe it?"

To my horror, half the class started laughing! Trent even piped in, "Hey Holly, that will teach you to pick me as your partner next time. I can promise you, I can read really good."

"Yeah, you're right. I'm sorry Trent. We should have been partners."

My teacher stood there with her mouth hanging open. "Class, you should be ashamed of yourselves." And out of the room my teacher stormed in search of the new kid.

CHAPTER 4

"Holly!" I snapped. "How could you call him that? Especially to his face!"

"Awe, come on, Cat. You're not up to your goody-two-shoe self again, helping all the *poor kids that are being picked on.*"

"Holly, that was so mean. He's new! It's got to be hard for him."

"Get real," I heard Trent say. "If he's in the eighth grade and can't read, I promise you, we aren't the first ones to tease him. I mean, come on, did you hear him? He sounded so stupid when he read."

"You mean *tried* to read!" Holly added laughing.

Just then the bell rang, and school was over. We all rushed out of the room, and instead of going straight to my locker, I rushed to my friends.

"Guys!"

"Hey, Cat!" Becky exclaimed, smiling. But after seeing my face, she lost her smile.

"What's wrong?" she asked. I was so mad that I thought my insides were going to burst. I looked at them and had to do a really quick summary of what had happened, because they all had to get on the bus.

"What? That's awful!" Dallas yelled out.

"I know, I'm so mad." I tightened my hands into fists.

"Hey, we have to get on the bus, but why don't you text us later."

Frustrated because we didn't have much time, I said, "Okay, maybe we need a group get together this weekend."

Just then the bell rang, signaling that the buses were coming.

"Sounds great, but gotta go!" They all yelled and rushed to their buses.

As I watched them walk off, a new fear came over me. Next week, that would be me rushing to get on the bus. We were moving into our new house this weekend.

As I walked back to my locker, my sister was standing there grinning at me.

"What's up with you, pouty face?"

"Nothing," I mumbled.

"Yeah, right. Why do you have that scowl on your face?"

"Because, I was just thinking, next week we will be riding in *the dungeon.*"

"What the heck is 'the dungeon'?"

I looked at her and got right in her face and exclaimed, "The school bus!"

Later that weekend the whole gang came over. We were all sitting on the floor in my room. Boxes were everywhere as they were helping me pack.

"So, how do you think we could help Jonah?" Becky asked as she folded up my sweatshirts to place in a moving box.

"I don't know. I was thinking that I might try to help teach him to read." With a sigh I asked, "What do you guys think about that?"

"That's a great idea, Cat! Maybe I could come too!" My sister said as she pulled all my junk from under my bed out to pack.

"Yeah, maybe. Thanks, sis."

"Um, guys?" Tyler spoke up. "What if he doesn't want your help?"

The room got as quiet as our library at school.

I asked, "Why wouldn't he want my help?"

"Yeah, if Cat can help teach him to read, then maybe he won't get teased anymore." Dallas said.

Tyler just shrugged his shoulders. "I don't know, just a thought."

"Well," Grace stood up and stretched, "I don't know about you guys, but I could really use a break."

"Great, what did you make?" Tyler asked.

Grace was the baker in my family. She would always find some kind of reason to bake, anything from friends coming over to getting an "A" on a test. The smells of cookies and brownies always filled our home. But today she surprised us all.

"Since we're celebrating moving, I made something special." She jumped up all excited.

"What is it?" Dallas asked.

"A chocolate cookie dessert!" She announced proudly.

"Yay!" I yelled, jumping up myself. "My favorite!"

"What's that?" Dallas asked, pausing with a box in her arms.

"It's our family's favorite. I layer a pan with crushed up cookies, ice cream, and a hot fudge topping."

"Wait!" I exclaimed. I held onto my lamp, as I prepared to box it up. "Did you use my favorite ice cream?"

"Yes, you know I would!"

Then we both yelled out at the same time and fist bumped, "Mackinac Island Fudge!"

"Yay! I love that kind." Tyler's eyes filled with excitement.

Becky was already running out of my room, but I heard her yell back, "Oh my gosh! My mouth is already watering!"

As we rushed out, I looked back and saw that Tyler was standing there, excitement gone, with a sadness that took over.

"What?" I asked and paused.

Tyler looked at me and answered, "Nothing's wrong. It just made me think back to when my dad left, and my mom just stayed in bed all day."

Tyler's dad had left just over a year ago, and his mom had gotten so sad that she would stay in bed all day and not take care of Tyler. She is so much better now, but sometimes I would still see the sadness in Tyler's eyes when he would think about it.

I turned to Tyler, so I could respond, but he looked at me at the same time, and our eyes connected, and I started to see stars...

CHAPTER 5

Tyler was sitting on his mom's bed telling her how his day went at school. He mentioned that his birthday was the next day.

"Oh honey! I'm so sorry, I forgot."

With shoulders slumped, Tyler mumbled, "It's okay, Mom."

Trying to sit up she said, "No it's not. Don't you worry. I will have something for you tomorrow. Now, what do you want for a dessert?"

Without having to think, Tyler rattled off his favorite dessert. "I want the chocolate cookie dessert."

"Oh, how could I forget? I used to make that for you all the time. It's always been your favorite."

"I know."

"Okay, don't you worry. Tomorrow when you get home from school, there will be a dessert waiting for you!"

Not knowing if his mom would really do it, he answered, "Okay Mom, but it's alright if you can't."

"Don't you worry." Then she looked right at him and added, "I promise."

The next day Tyler ran from the bus to his house in anticipation for his birthday dessert. Dropping his backpack, he didn't find anything on the table. He opened the freezer door to see if she had put it there, but to his sadness, there was no dessert.

Looking around the room, it was empty of not only a dessert, but of any presents.

Tyler then walked slowly to his own room and mumbled, "Happy birthday to me," and shut the door.

I shook my head to clear the vision. I was completely speechless. I had no idea what to even say. I felt so bad for him.

Tyler saw me staring at him and had a question in his eyes.

"Cat? You okay?"

"Um, yeah. I'm fine. You know if we wait much longer, they may have the whole dessert gone before we get any of it."

That got his feet moving. And as we sat around the table enjoying the treat, everyone was talking and laughing at the same time. Well, everyone but Tyler. He sat there, dessert half gone. He wasn't talking to anyone, just busy eating. He had his eyes closed, enjoying every single bite.

CHAPTER 6

The next day was moving day. Even though it was almost the end of November in Michigan, I'd been sweating all morning. Going up and down the steps carrying boxes was wearing me out.

"Come on, Cat!" Grace said excitedly. "Dad said we're ready to take another load to the new house."

"Coming." I yelled, carrying a box of my candles and knickknacks I had in my room.

As we pulled up to our new house I saw Jonah coming towards us.

"Need any help?"

"Sure," my dad said. "If you could help carry boxes into the house and put them in the living room, that would be great! Thanks."

Jonah shrugged. "No problem."

And to my and Grace's amazement, Jonah started carrying the boxes at a super-fast speed.

"Cat! Did you see that?"

"See what?" I tried to play dumb.

"Jonah! He carried the box like it was a feather, and you and I both had to carry that box out to the car together!"

"So?"

I watched as that silly look took over Grace's face again. "Did you see his muscles?"

Rolling my eyes, I swatted her on the arm. "Good grief. No, I did not see his muscles. For one," I pointed out. "He's wearing a coat! *And*," I added as I walked away, "I wasn't looking."

"Hmph," I heard Grace say. "You wouldn't recognize beauty if it kicked you in the butt!" she yelled back.

That got me laughing. I was still laughing when Jonah came back out for another box.

"What's so funny?" he asked.

"Oh, Grace and I were just talking." I paused and looked over my shoulder at my sister. She was standing behind Jonah frantically waving her hands in the air, shaking her head at me. All the while she had a panicked look on her face.

"Well," I continued with a smile, "Grace was just admiring all the beauty around here." I said with a wink in her direction.

I heard my mom yell from the car, "Okay, Grace, less admiring and more working!"

With her face as red as my sweatshirt, Grace ran over and grabbed the box from my mom's arms and rushed into the house.

As the day went on, I couldn't believe how hard Jonah worked. Grace and I had to keep taking breaks, but he seemed to never stop.

His only breaks were when Grace would offer him yet another brownie or cookie. He finally had to start passing on her treats.

"I think I'm sugared out for one day, but thank you. They were great."

My sister was floating around the rest of the day. Me? I was on a mission. I noticed Jonah was really nice, and a very hard worker. I wanted to do something for him. I was determined more than ever to help him read. I just wasn't sure how to do it.

Later that night as I lay in my new room, with boxes all around me, I thought back to when Jonah was trying to read with Holly. Everyone had been laughing at him.

Yup, I was going to help him. I was going to change him. Then, just maybe he wouldn't get teased as much. So, as I lay in bed, I searched my phone until my eyes grew heavy and closed. The last thing I remembered in my mind was the site I had clicked on, *"How to teach a child to read."*

CHAPTER 7

As Monday came, my parents said that for the first day in our new house they would take us to school, but tomorrow would be different. I sat in first-hour with my friends talking until the bell rang. As we all found our seats my teacher began talking.

"Class, I just got asked to direct the school play! Isn't that exciting?"

"Ha!" Trent yelled out.

Mrs. Hill scowled at him.

"Sorry," he mumbled. "Just won't be in any stupid play."

"What I was going to say was, I may need help with making some of the props."

"Oh, that sounds like fun!"

"Good, thank you Becky. I could use some of you to paint for me, but..." she paused, "what I really need is a high platform built. We are doing a Christmas play, so we need a tower for the North Pole. Do any of you have any idea how we could do that? I'm not very good with wood, nails, and hammers."

"You could ask the shop teacher." Dallas suggested.

"That's a great idea. Maybe he would have some students that could think of something."

Out of the back of the room, I heard a quiet voice begin to talk. "Or, you could just...."

And on and on went the ideas of what type of wood, nails, how to cut the wood, at which angles, and so on.

The whole class, including Mrs. Hill, turned to look at who had just spoken. Jonah sat there red-faced. Mrs. Hill smiled. "Well class, I think we found our man. Jonah, I am putting you in charge of making the tower for the school play."

"Me?" he asked.

"Yes, definitely, and," looking around the room, "if you need help just grab some other students to help you."

"Yeah," Holly piped in, studying her perfectly-painted-pale-pink nails. "He's going to need all the help he can get, (looking at him) with reading the directions!" That brought laughter, not only from Holly but half the class.

"Holly," Mrs. Hill sternly demanded, "out in the hall, *now*."

Acting all innocent, she responded, "What? Me? What did I do?" Pausing with a pout, "I was just joking around."

"I said, out."

And that was where Holly stayed for the rest of the hour.

As soon as the bell rang, my friends and I all rushed to Jonah.

"We'll help you."

"Thanks," he responded shyly. "I didn't mean she had to pick me, I was just telling her what I thought she could do."

"But it sounds like you know what you're talking about." Tyler said.

"Well, it won't be that hard. It's easy really. Thanks for the help."

"Yeah, well, I'm not sure how much help we'll be, but we'll sure try." Dallas added.

"It will be no big deal. If you guys could just help me hammer and cut some wood, that would be great."

We all just stood there and looked at each other, then back at him.

"Yeah, about that," Becky started. Pulling on her sweatshirt strings she continued, "I can't speak for all the others, but the last time I tried to hammer a nail, the only nail I hit was my finger nail, and it turned black and blue and eventually fell off!"

"Maybe we could help you more with holding the wood, instead of cutting it. Last time I tried to help my mom cut a piece of wood, we ended up back at the hardware store, asking for a new piece, and having them cut it for us." Tyler sheepishly looked down, "I kind of cut it to four inches instead of four feet."

Jonah looked at us as if we were from another planet. "Are you guys serious?"

"Pretty much!" Dallas responded.

"Oh, okay. Well then, maybe you can just hold the wood or something like that, I guess."

As we walked out of the classroom, I felt kinda dumb. Here was the student who couldn't read a chapter, but give him a hammer and nail, and he was all set. We could all read, but ask us to build something? We didn't have a clue.

Not a single clue.

CHAPTER 8

As I got home from school, I decided today was the day. The day I was going to try and help Jonah learn to read. I set my backpack down, unzipped it and grabbed the book that I had checked out from the library. I knew it would work because I had googled it and read up on how to teach a kindergartener to read.

As I yelled over my shoulder, I called out to my mom and Grace, "I'll be right back. Just saying 'hi' to our neighbors."

"Oh, I'm so coming!" hollered Grace.

Putting up my hand to stop her I told her, "Not today, Grace." I whispered in her ear, "I'm going to teach Jonah how to read, so I think I should do it alone, so he doesn't feel stupid."

Crossing her arms over her stomach she stomped off, "You just want him for yourself."

Rolling my eyes, I started to walk out the door, but I didn't get very far before Grace ran and caught up to me.

"Please at least give him a cookie I made."

"Okay, but where's the one for me?"

"Hmph, you don't get one, since you won't let me come with you." With a pout, she turned to walk off.

"Fine." I said, smiling, "I'll just eat this one." And I pretended to take a bite.

"Wait!" She yelled. "Okay, fine, I'll go get you one, but next time, promise to bring me along."

"I promise."

With two cookies in hand, I knocked on their red painted door. Jonah's mom answered.

"Oh, hi, Cat. This is a nice surprise."

"I was wondering if Jonah was home from school?"

"Yes, he's in his room working on homework. You can go on in. Second door on the left."

"Thanks."

After I knocked, he told me I could come in. I handed him his cookie and he smiled.

Seeing papers all over his bed I asked, "What are you working on?"

Shrugging his shoulders, he started to collect his papers.

"Nothing, just some homework."

"Yeah, I've got some too." I plopped on the end of the bed, "How are you liking school so far?"

"It's okay I guess."

"Well, it sounds like building the tower thingy for the play will be fun."

"Yeah, I'm excited about that."

We just sat there, I didn't know what to say.

"Well," I grabbed my bag and pulled out the book I had gotten. "I just thought maybe I could help you out and teach you to read." And quickly added, "So Holly and Trent will stop teasing you."

I noticed that I was starting to talk fast because I was nervous. I had the book open on my lap and I started flipping through the pages.

"So, the internet said if I start at the beginning of this book, that by the time we are done with it you will be a fantastic reader!"

I jumped as a hand slammed down on the page. I looked up into a very red, very angry face.

He leaned towards me and bit out, "I...don't...want...or...need...your...help"

And my very round eyes met his very angry eyes, and I started to see stars...

CHAPTER 9

There was Jonah sitting at his kitchen table with his mom.

"It says here you need to write a one-page report on the Empire State Building." His mom said as she gripped his homework sheet in her hands.

"What? I can't write a whole page paper, Mom!"

"I know son," letting out a big sigh his mom added, "I'll help you."

"But, you *always* have to help me. You spend every night helping me do my homework." Frustrated, he pushed his paper aside and slouched in his chair.

"Face it," he mumbled. "I'm just dumb."

"No, you're not! Don't ever say that again!"

"Come on, Mom! You're just saying that because you're my mom."

"No, I'm not. I'm saying it because it's true."

"Look at me, I can't read. What's wrong with me? I just want to be normal, like everyone else." His voice squeaked in desperation.

Just then his little sister came bouncing into the room.

"Look Mommy, I can read!" and she crawled up into her mommy's lap and placed the book on the table.

"Where did you get that?" Jonah growled.

"In your room, I found it." She said in her sweet angelic voice.

"You're not supposed to be in my room."

I know, but I was walking by and I saw the book. Watch!" And she opened the book and read with sheer confidence, "The cat had a bat..."

"Great!" Jonah jumped up and walked off grunting out, "My seven-year-old baby sister can read better than me. This life sucks." And off he went and slammed his bedroom door shut.

"Why's Jonah so mad at me mommy?" his little sister, River asked.

"Oh, sweetheart," and she hugged her daughter tightly. "Your brother's not mad at you." She turned her daughter, who was still in her lap, around to look at her as she replied, "Your brother loves you very much, but do you remember when you get sad sometimes?"

Nodding her head, she answered, "Yeah, like when Bobby at school pulls my hair?"

"Um, something like that. Well, your brother is sad."

"How come?"

"Well," trying to think of a way to explain it to a seven-year-old, she continued, "sometimes he thinks he's not a smart person. Sometimes kids will be mean and call him names, and it makes his heart very sad. So, when he feels that way, it looks like he is angry, but really he's embarrassed and hurting."

She could tell her daughter was thinking it over in her little head. Not knowing what River would say, she was surprised when two little hands gently touched both her cheeks.

"Mommy," River leaned forward until their noses were almost touching.

"What honey?" her mother answered.

"I think Jonah is the bestest brother in the whole wide world."

With her eyes stinging from unshed tears, her mom answered, "I know honey, you are so right."

River leaned in and kissed the end of her mommy's nose and wiggled out of her embrace.

"Where are you going honey?"

Twirling around, Jonah's little sister looked surprised that her mom didn't know.

"I'm going to give Jonah a hug. A big bear hug. They always help me when I'm sad."

"That's so sweet, honey. Can you give him a kiss from me too?"

"What?" She twirled around to face her mom. "*A kiss?*"

Grabbing the doorknob that led to her brother's room, she added, "Gross! I'm not kissing a *boy*! They've got cooties!"

And into the room she disappeared.

"I'm sorry Jonah," I answered, hopping up from the bed.

"Just go please."

"But... I just wanted to help." I pleaded. As he got up from the bed he walked to his door and held it open. I think that was my hint to leave. This had all gone wrong. As I slowly walked out of his room I heard him growl, "I don't want or need your help."

And that was it. I walked home feeling awful.

CHAPTER 10

By the next morning, I felt even more depressed than the day before at Jonah's house. I not only had Jonah mad at me, I had to stand here, in the cold, watching and waiting. This would probably go down in history as the worst day of my life. As I waited for the school bus to come around the corner, I realized something. I was *terrified.*

I looked to my left and there stood Grace. She talked non-stop to Jonah with that dreamy look on her face. Jonah didn't make waiting for the bus any easier. We hadn't spoken since I left his house yesterday. I decided to just take a quick peek his way, hoping he wouldn't see me. As I slowly turned my head my eyes settled on his face. At the same time, he looked my way. With a frown, he just as quickly turned away.

Letting out a big sigh, I turned and just stood there. How did I mess this up so badly? I thought my life had fallen apart.

"There it is!" Grace exclaimed, with a little too much excitement for a morning.

My heart felt like it had just pumped right out of my winter coat and flew away. Okay, I shouldn't have worn such a thick coat today. I think I actually had sweat running down my face. Even though it had been an extra cold November day with heavy winds, I heated up like an oven that had just cooked a turkey on Thanksgiving Day.

And there it was. So big and yellow. Like a huge bumble bee coming to sting me. The pain and horror of a bee sting would have been better than this. I could not ignore the screeching of the brakes as the bus slowed to our house. Next, the unmistakable "pop" sound all busses made when they came to a complete stop.

"Clank," went the door as it opened.

I started to take a step forward when I felt a hand gently clasp my arm. I looked up just as Jonah shook his head at me.

"Not yet," he said quietly and gently.

I was very confused. But then I heard over a microphone that had come from the bus, "*you may cross now.*"

Jonah just as gently released my arm, gave me the gesture to go first, and followed me across the road.

As I reached the door opening, I just stared at the steps. Taking a deep breath, I took one step at a time.

Expecting to walk onto a bus full of loud, hyper kids throwing paper balls everywhere, I was very pleased and surprised to see a very quiet bus.

People were just looking out the windows or had headphones on.

"Woah, I could handle this." I mumbled to myself. As I looked around, I found an open seat next to a girl in my grade that I had never spoken to before.

"Can I sit here?" I asked.

She grabbed her backpack and motioned for me to sit.

As the ride began, I didn't know if I was supposed to talk to the girl or just stay quiet. I looked down the aisle and saw Grace sitting with Jonah. I could see she talked a mile a minute, but I couldn't tell if Jonah listened to her or not.

Letting out a sigh, I took a peek at the girl sitting next to me. She was gazing out the window. I had never talked to her before. Really, hardly anyone had ever talked to her before. Everyone said she was so stuck up because she wouldn't speak or look at others.

I was just about to pull out my phone when I remembered our janitor's words. We had an assembly a couple of weeks ago, and he told us he wanted us to become treasure seekers. He asked if we would not listen to what others said about people, reach out and get to know them instead. He wanted us to see who they were on the inside. He had told us that we might find a treasure in that person.

I smiled as I remembered back to when Mr. Williams challenged all of us to think of what that treasure would be when we found it in a person. Becky had figured out the answer and she was so excited. When Becky told Mr. Williams that the treasure you found in a person was *a friend*, I literally thought she was going to burst when he told us that Becky had guessed the right answer.

Okay, snapping back to the present, I snuck a quick peek at Eva sitting next to me. If I was going to be a treasure seeker, then I had to ignore the rumors I had always heard about her and try to be nice. Really, how hard could it be to say "hi" to someone?

"Hi," I said anticipating her response.

Nothing. Absolutely nothing.

CHAPTER 11

I couldn't believe it! She didn't even respond to me. Maybe all those rumors were right, and she was a stuck-up snob. Should I give her another chance? Ugh, it'd be a lot easier if I just ignored her. I mean, she did it to me. But there was a voice in my head that told me I should try again.

Clearing my throat loudly, I tried again, "Hi."

Her head snapped around and she looked at me. It was then that I saw earbuds in both her ears. Pulling them out she shyly asked, "I'm sorry, did you say something?"

"I just said, hi."

"Oh," she turned a couple of shades redder, then added, "Hi, I'm sorry about that, I didn't hear you."

I saw that as soon as she finished talking, she dipped her head down, which caused her long, brown, golden-streaked hair to fall over her shoulders and cover her face. Even though she didn't talk to anyone, we all knew she was the prettiest girl in our grade. Probably the prettiest in the whole school.

Even though her hair reached down her back, I knew it hid very blue eyes, with a flawless face. Great, I had just woken up with a zit right in the middle of my forehead this morning. My friends and I had all been breaking out since last year, but I didn't think Eva ever had one single pimple.

Maybe that was why she thought she was too good for us. While kids in my grade had zits, glasses, and braces, this girl looked like she just came out of a model magazine.

I reached up and tried to adjust my hair to see if it would cover my pimple. I really tried not to touch it, but it was still so red. I felt like if anyone looked at me, their eyes would be drawn to my forehead, like it glowed or something.

With all of my crazy, frizzy hair all one length, it just fell back to the side. Great, maybe I needed to get bangs. Maybe then it would cover up my zits.

Treasure seeker, okay, as I tried to adjust my hair one more time, I decided I would try to talk to her again.

"This is my first time on this bus. We just moved into a different house. I used to walk to school every day." I found myself talking as much as Grace. Great, she probably thought I was crazy, but for some reason my mouth had a mind of its own.

"Do you ride every day?" I didn't even give her time to answer. "There's another family who just moved in next door to us. That boy up there with my sister," pointing their way, "my sister is *in love* with him. She thinks he's *so hot*." I rolled my eyes and I finally paused and looked over at my bus seat partner.

To my surprise, Eva was shyly smiling at me.

"Sorry, I don't usually talk this much. That is usually saved for my sister. I've never met someone who can talk as much, or as fast as her."

I heard giggling, so I turned and looked at Eva. She had actually laughed. I couldn't believe it. I had never heard a laugh from her before. I guess my non-stop talking had kept her entertained, so I continued.

"So, do you like riding the bus?" I waited for her to say something but found myself disappointed when she quickly turned away.

Well, I tried. I couldn't help it if she won't talk to me. I wiggled in my seat, trying to get comfortable, when I heard a very faint, "No."

I couldn't tell if it had really been Eva who had talked, so I looked her way.

Then our eyes connected, and I started to see stars...

Eva was sitting on the bus, and Trent was sitting with her. "So," Trent started, "you want to hang out sometime?"

Eva just kept staring out the window.

"What's wrong, Trent? The pretty girl isn't falling for your good looks?" A boy in the seat behind snickered.

"Shut up, Brenden."

"Hey, Eva," Trent tried again. "You know you're the hottest girl in our school."

"Don't let Holly hear you say that!"

"I said, shut up Brenden!"

Eva just shifted closer to the window. A girl in a seat across from Trent added, "She's just a snob.

Doesn't talk to anyone, she thinks she's better than everyone else."

"Yeah," Brenden added, "too bad she's so cute. Cute, but a snob, total jerk."

"Yeah," Trent agreed, "loser."

At that the bus pulled up to the school, and they all jumped out of their seats and left Eva sitting in her seat all alone. After the bus cleared out, Eva slowly stood up and grabbed her backpack, but not before I could see the shaking of her hands. Eva was not a snob, she was petrified.

I looked her way and saw her shaking her head, "No, I don't like riding the bus."

Just then I heard her phone ding. She looked down at it and I saw her face drain of all color. Her usually rosy pink cheeks were now pasty white.

"What's wrong? Are you okay?"

"Um, I'm fine."

She then slumped down and looked out the window.

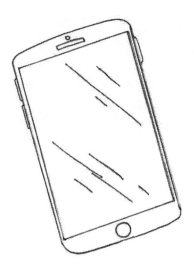

Someone must have just sent her a mean text. Who could it be? Were Holly

and Trent on the move again? Didn't
they leave anyone alone?

CHAPTER 12

I walked into first-hour, and I headed straight to my desk.

"Hey Cat, how was the bus?" Becky asked.

"Better than I thought it would be." I answered truthfully. I just couldn't get Eva's sad face out of my head.

"Okay class, everyone take your seats."

It was the first time I really looked at my teacher. What in the world was she wearing?

"What are you wearing?" Holly expressed my exact thoughts.

"Oh, I'm wearing an elf costume. I'm trying to get you kids excited about the play. I was hoping we would get a bigger turnout this year." She answered as she grinned ear to ear.

She had on a green and red elf outfit. It had white fuzzy fur around the collar, wrist and ankles. And it was decorated with bells on the hat and toes of the shoes. As she talked, the hat flopped in front of her and the bell landed against her cheek.

"Um, I don't think that's going to help your cause." Holly snickered.

Ignoring the comment, my teacher went on, "I would like to talk about building the tower." She looked straight at Jonah and asked, "Will you be willing to build it for me, like we talked about the other day?"

"Sure, sounds like fun." Jonah responded.

"Fun? Get all hot and sweaty, break a nail? Lots of fun there Jonah." Holly laughed, along with others in the class. Ugh, this was so frustrating. I just couldn't figure out how to help him.

"Great, thanks Jonah," Our teacher responded. "Now, I've assigned Dallas, Cat, Becky, and Tyler to help you build it. If you need anything just ask me, okay?"

"Okay, thanks."

Great. I could help him read, but he didn't want my help. Now, he could use my help, but I didn't have a clue what I would be doing. Not a single clue.

Once home, my mom called me into the living room.

"Hey honey, I was just wondering how you were doing?"

"Fine." I said.

"Well, yesterday when you got home from Jonah's house you looked a little sad. Then this morning going to the bus you looked absolutely terrified."

"Oh, that. Well, I don't get it mom. Jonah can't read well, and I went over to help him. I got a book and everything, thinking I could teach him."

"And how did that go?"

"Not too well. He kinda got mad, really mad at me. His face turned all red and everything."

"What did he say?"

"He said he doesn't want my help."

"Hmm, that's what I was afraid of."

"What do you mean? I could really help him, Mom. Then he wouldn't get teased so much."

"Honey, I know you were trying to help, but I've talked with his mom. He's had so much help from teachers, specialists, and so on. You trying to help him will do more harm than good."

"Why?"

"Because, honey. It probably makes him feel embarrassed, that a kid his age is trying to fix him."

"I'm trying to help him, not fix him."

"I know, but to him, it probably feels the same."

"Then what do I do?"

"Be a friend."

"I'm trying."

"No, like him as a friend for who he is today. Not for who you want him to be, or who you think he should be."

"I don't get it."

"He has had a lot of professionals try to help him, he just needs someone to come alongside him and be a friend, for who he is. Not being able to read and all. Don't try to change him."

"But, Mom, he's different than the rest of us."

"Honey, sometimes different is good. Didn't you say the janitor, Mr.

Williams, was wanting you kids to search deeper into others?"

"Yes, we're supposed to be treasure seekers."

"Well, here's your chance. Spend time just being nice to him. You may find that being different can be a very good thing. You may be surprised at what you discover."

Leaning over, I gave my mom a big hug. "Thanks, Mom. I needed that. I will stop trying to fix him, and just hang out with him, as he is."

"Good." My mom released me, and added, "How about you go do your homework, and then help me make dinner tonight."

"Okay, sounds good."

And off I went to my new room to start working on my math homework.

Walking down the hall I passed Grace's room. Our rooms were right next to each other, so I peeked my head in. I could see Grace sitting at her white desk with all hot pink accessories. Even the pen she was using had a hot pink fuzzy end to it.

"Hey Grace, how did you like riding the bus today?"

Whirling around she answered, "Are you serious? I got to sit by Jonah, so to answer your question, *it was great!*"

"Good, what did you think of the girl I was sitting with? Eva is her name."

"Oh, she's alright I guess."

"What do you mean, 'alright'? I talked to her today and she seemed nice."

"Well, I think she's kinda stuck up, but if you want to talk to her, then have fun."

I thought my sister might have been joking but looking at her face I realized she wasn't. What in the world was wrong with her? I've never seen her like this before.

Walking off, I figured Grace was probably sitting in her room doing her homework, daydreaming about how cute Jonah was. While I would be in my room, doing my homework, having my mind drift as well. Not about how cute he was, but how I could fix the damage I had done.

Or was I too late? Had I already wrecked our new friendship?

CHAPTER 13

A couple hours later, we had eaten dinner and Grace and I had started cleaning up the kitchen. I looked up from wiping the table when I heard a knock at the door.

"He's here." I heard my dad say, as he walked towards the door.

My sister and I exchanged looks. Who was here?

"Hi Jonah, come on in."

"What?" I looked at Grace and she threw her dish towel down and started to rush off.

"Wait!" I yelled back.

"What?" She asked whipping around.

"Where are you going? We aren't done drying the dishes."

"Are you kidding? I'm going to check my hair!"

And off she went. Shaking my head, I couldn't help but smile. Grace had the biggest crush on Jonah, but little did she know, the big eighth grader probably didn't even notice the little sixth grader.

"Hi, Cat."

"Oh, hi Jonah." Clinging to the dishrag in my hands, I leaned my hip against the counter. I was trying to act all normal on the outside, when my heart was beating as fast as a race car. I had no idea if he was still mad at me. He didn't talk to me at school today but kept to himself.

"What are you doing here? I didn't know you were coming over tonight." I was just so happy right now that he was actually talking to me.

"Your dad asked if I could help him make up some plans for a new tree house for you and your sister."

"Oh! Great." But then my shoulders slumped. "But, we have no trees. The whole yard is bare."

"That's okay, we can work around that." He said with a half grin.

Okay, I didn't think he hated me. I mean, I got part of a grin out of his face.

"How is that going to work? How can you build a treehouse with no trees?"

"Well, that's the cool part. My dad always says, *'where there's a will, there's a way.'*"

There was an awkward silence that followed. I looked down at the rag in my hands.

"Hey Cat," he said in a low voice.

I looked up to see him focused on me.

"What?" I gulped. I knew he was probably going to yell at me, I just didn't know if I could handle it.

Looking around to make sure it was just the two of us, he added, "I just wanted to tell you that I'm sorry about yesterday."

"It's okay."

"No, I've struggled my whole life with reading, and I've had so many people try to help me." With a sad chuckle, he added, "I actually had a teacher go through the same book you had yesterday."

Shocked, but feeling awful, I responded, "I'm so sorry. I wasn't trying to hurt you."

"I know you weren't, and I shouldn't have gotten so mad. When I get embarrassed I take it out as if I'm mad at you, but I'm madder at myself. I'm sorry."

"How about we start over?" I suggested.

"Sounds great." Then with a tug of a smile that reached his eyes he held out his hand and said, "Hi, my name is Jonah."

Playing along, I grabbed his hand to shake it and heard myself say, "Hi, I'm Cat. I heard we're neighbors."

Just then my sister walked into the room and saw our hands together. She froze and stood there with her mouth hanging open. Just as quickly as I grabbed his hand to give it a shake, I released it.

"Hey Grace, guess what? Dad asked Jonah to come over to help make plans for the tree house."

Looking back and forth between us, she responded, "Oh, that's great." But her excitement didn't reach her voice.

I started to laugh. I couldn't believe Grace would think I liked him. Thinking about it more, I started to laugh harder. I bet she was just fuming with me and couldn't wait to talk to me alone. Oh shoot, my laughter was starting to come from deep within.

"Uh oh," Grace said looking over at Jonah. "My sister is losing it."

Just then my dad walked in the room.

"Hey kids, come sit down, I want you girls to give Jonah and I an idea of what you are wanting the new treehouse to look like." Looking over at me with a question in his eyes, he turned and asked the other two, "Um, what's wrong with Cat?"

Shrugging his shoulders Jonah answered, "Um, I have no idea sir. She started laughing, and she won't stop." Shifting uncomfortably, he added, "I see tears coming out of her eyes, do you think she's okay?"

"Well," my dad went on, "Jonah, welcome to a house full of girls. She will be just fine, you just have to wait it out." And my dad ended his sentence with a huge grin.

Calming myself down I went to the table and plopped down. "Okay," I answered, and looked towards Grace. It was the first time I had looked at her since she ran out of the room. Holy cow, she had pulled her hair back and left little wispies hanging around her face. Narrowing my eyes, I asked her, "Are you wearing makeup? And did you just curl-"

I couldn't finish my sentence because she butted in, "I'm ready dad, let's get started."

With papers laid out across the table, my dad asked us what we would like for our tree house.

"How do you make it with no trees?" Grace asked. My thoughts exactly.

"We will use wood. It will be more like a tall fort. Instead of a tree holding it up, we will have legs of wood."

"Cool!" Grace exclaimed.

We spent the next half hour going over what we would like.

My dad asked if Jonah would like to go with us to the home improvement store this weekend to pick out all of the materials. He agreed very quickly and with an excitement I couldn't understand.

CHAPTER 14

Saturday morning came bright and early. I woke to a knock on my door. At first, I thought I was dreaming, but since the knock wouldn't go away I realized it was real. Groaning, I rolled my head to see the clock. Eight o'clock.

"Come in!" I yelled groggily.

With my door flying open, Grace came barreling over to my bed. "Cat! Time to get up!"

"It's eight o'clock in the morning on a Saturday. Why do I have to get up?"

"Don't you remember? We're going to the store with dad and Jonah."

Ugh, "I forgot. Why so early?"

"This is not early. Seriously. I don't know how you ever sleep in till eleven on Saturdays anyway." She jumped back up and headed to the door, while yelling over her shoulder, "Hurry up, Dad's stopping to get us donuts and cider on the way!" And off she went down the hall.

I laid there looking around at my new room. At least I got to keep my same bed. It was so cozy that I had such a hard time getting out of it. I could tell the days and nights were getting a lot colder and snow would be coming soon.

Snuggling deeper into my fluffy bedspread, I was just about to doze off again, when I heard my sister yell, "Cat! You better not be falling back to sleep!"

"Shoot," I threw my warm comfy covers off and stepped onto soft, new carpet. So glad we didn't have hardwood floors. They were so cold in the winter. I grabbed my favorite ripped jeans and navy blue baggy sweatshirt. I threw them on and headed to the bathroom to throw my hair up for the day. I believe in comfy clothes all the way on a Saturday. Well, any day for me. I love my sweatshirts.

Entering the kitchen, I was greeted by my dad, Grace, and Jonah.

"Okay, everyone ready?"

"Yes, we're all set." Grace exclaimed.

As we headed to the car, Grace and I took the back seat of my dad's truck, while Jonah sat up front.

After a quick stop to grab the donuts and cider, we were on our way to the store.

As we entered I looked all around. Wow, was this store big. I couldn't believe it. How did anyone find anything?

"Okay, we are going to need a lot of materials. Jonah, can you and Cat take this list and start getting everything on it, and Grace and I will grab everything else?"

"Sure, no problem." And Jonah and I headed off, but not before seeing Grace's shocked face. I think she would have traded places with me in a heartbeat.

"Okay, your dad needs a few different types of nails. Can you help me find them?"

"Uh, do you have a picture of what they look like, or something?"

Looking at me strangely, he responded, "A picture? That would be a no. I do have the size we need, so we just look for that."

Feeling a little stupid I added, "Oh, okay, sure."

As we collected items off the list, I realized this was way out of my element. I had no idea what we were getting. I wasn't any help. All I did was push the cart. Jonah, on the other hand, seemed like he was in a candy store. He was so excited and knew what he was looking for.

Standing back as he looked at some items, I just watched him. Even though he had a hard time reading, man could he do other things. Maybe my mom was right. I didn't have to change him, he was just better at different things than me.

So, I just continued to push the cart the rest of the trip, while Jonah checked off the items one at a time.

"When are we going to start building it?" I asked.

With his face fully concentrating on a board, he answered without looking up, "Today, when we get back."

"Today? That's fast. Are you going to help too?"

Now, that got his attention. "Of course, I am. I wouldn't miss this for the world. I love this stuff."

He looked up at me and asked, "Hey, I'm all done with the list, I saw that they had a lot of Halloween stuff on clearance. Do you want to go check it out?"

"Sure, why not. Then we can see if we see Dad and Grace on the way."

"Great!"

So, we headed to all the Halloween items on sale. I didn't know why he wanted to look at it all, but once I got over there I could see why. They had huge blow up ghosts, spiders, and much more.

"Hey, check this out!" Jonah said all muffled.

I looked over and he was wearing this freaky mask with fake scars and blood all over it.

"Eww, gross, that's disgusting."

As he laughed, he pulled it off and kept looking.

I had been looking at some cute plastic pumpkin faces when I heard Jonah yell out, "Watch out!"

All of a sudden, this huge black, furry spider fell in front of my face! I screamed and ran down the aisle, all the while frantically wiping my face and arms.

"Is it on me?" I yelled. "Is it on me?"

Jonah couldn't even answer me because he was laughing so hard. I turned back around and found the spider he had thrown at me. It was a fake fuzzy looking dark black spider, the size of a softball.

"That was so not funny!" I scolded him.

He continued to laugh.

"Stop! It's not funny, that really scared me!" I was horrified to hear a chuckle escape my lips.

"You have to admit," he said between bursts of laughter, "it was hilarious!"

"Hmph," I said, and turned to watch as Grace and my Dad headed our way.

"You have a sick sense of humor." I yelled over my shoulder and grabbed the cart to go check out.

"What's going on?" Grace asked me.

"He's all yours, Grace, you can have him." I said as I walked off. "Your prince charming isn't very charming."

CHAPTER 15

Two hours later I found myself longing to be back in my warm, cozy house. We had gotten home from the hardware store and we started working right away. I had been outside for over an hour and I was freezing. I couldn't feel my fingers or toes anymore.

As I watched Jonah hold a board up, he pulled a large nail out of his tool belt. "Hey Cat, can you grab that hammer? While I hold up the board and nail, would you hammer it in for me?

Shocked with horror I asked, "Me? You want me to hammer it?" I couldn't hammer anything for the life of me, and my hands were frozen solid.

"Yeah," then he added all sweet like, "please?"

"You're not teasing me again, right?"

"Me? Tease? Never, I just need you to hammer this in for me."

I picked up the hammer and slowly walked over to where he was standing.

"Okay, all you have to do is hit the head of the nail."

"Alright." All of a sudden, the bitter cold outside felt like an oven.

Tap, tap, tap.

"Um, you can hit it a little harder than that." Jonah said with a smile.

WHAP!

"Ow! My finger!"

The next thing I knew, Jonah was bent over holding his hand, groaning in pain.

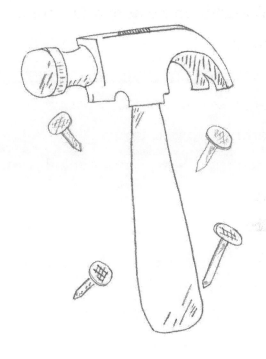

"I'm so sorry! I'm so sorry Jonah! I told you I couldn't use a hammer!"

To my surprise he stood up straight. A huge grin covered his face and he said, "Just kidding, you didn't hit me."

"What?" I exclaimed. "No way!" And I swatted his arm as hard as I could.

Just then I heard my dad burst out laughing, as Jonah joined right in.

I started to stomp off towards the house, as I mumbled, "Laugh all you want, that wasn't funny."

"Hey Cat." My dad yelled out in between bursts of laughter, "where are you going?"

"As far away from you two as possible!"

And off I went with a scowl on my face, which soon transformed into a smile. I couldn't keep a straight face, not when I could hear them in the background laughing and having a blast, while they built my treehouse.

***

The next morning on the bus, I looked for Eva. Instead of looking out the window, like she normally did, her eyes were focused right on me.

"Can I sit with you again?" I asked.

"Sure," as she pulled her backpack out of the way.

I noticed Jonah and Grace were sitting right in front of us.

"Hey guys, I want you to meet Eva."

They both turned around and Jonah said, "Hi Eva, it's nice to meet you."

She looked down shyly and added, "Yeah, you too."

I waited for Grace to say something, but she just turned around. What had gotten into her? She had been acting so strange lately. I'd have to talk to her sometime and see what was wrong.

"How are you liking school so far?" I asked Eva.

"It's okay, I'm not a big fan of it though. How about you?"

"Well, I think the best word to describe my year so far is 'interesting'."

"What do you mean?"

I couldn't tell her about my fall out of my old tree house which caused me to have visions. The only ones who knew about them were Grace, Tyler, Becky, and Dallas.

"I don't know, I guess I just have different friends this year."

"Hmm, I see people switch friends a lot. People seem to jump from group to group."

"Yeah, I guess so. I just got sick of my friends being so mean."

"Well, that's a good reason to find other friends."

I saw her give me a half smile. But it vanished when I asked the next question.

"Who are your friends? Who do you hang out with?"

She looked down at her lap, then up at me, and our eyes connected, and I started to see stars...

There was Eva, sitting in her room by herself painting a beautiful picture. With her pastel colors spread out and paintbrush moving, she peacefully made long flowing strokes while listening to music.

Ping, Ping, Ping.

"What in the world?"

She laid her paintbrush down, wiped her hands on her apron and turned down her radio.

Walking to the window she looked out to see some classmates down on the sidewalk. They were motioning for her to open her window.

Unlocking it, she pushed it up and leaned forward to see what they needed.

"Hey hermit! Whatcha doing up there all the time?"

"Yeah, don't you ever come out of that room?"

Then they looked at each other and started talking.

"Look at her, she doesn't even answer."

"I know. She's staring at us as if *we're* the crazy ones."

Looking back up at Eva, a boy replied, "Just to let you know, *you're* the crazy one! You can't even talk, can you?"

As she started to push her window shut, she heard a girl from the group yell out, "Yeah, just shut your window and hide away." Cupping her hands over her mouth to be sure Eva heard her she yelled, "Like you always do. *Freak*!"

And they continued to walk down the sidewalk, laughing.

Eva shut her window, rushed over to her seat and took deep breaths. She seemed to be almost having a panic attack. Calming herself, she stared at her painting, then took her brush and dipped it in black paint.

She smeared it all over her picture to destroy it.

"Why can't you be normal like them?" She started to cry into her hands. Reaching over to her little end table, she grabbed her hand mirror and looked at herself.

"Why do you have to be so shy! Why can't you talk to anyone?"

Turning her head away, she laid her mirror down and whispered, "You will never have any friends. You will always be alone."

Shaking my head to clear the vision, I heard her respond quietly.

"Um, I don't really know. I think friends are overrated."

CHAPTER 16

I looked and saw a math book sticking out of her backpack and an idea formed.

"Hey, I know we have a math test tomorrow and I am awful at math! Would you want to come over later today and study?"

"Really? Isn't it kinda hard to study for math?"

"No, I don't have a clue what I am doing in the class. Anything you can show me will help me on the test." I didn't know what she would say, but I was surprised when she agreed.

"Sure, I can ride my bike over after I get home."

"Great! I'll be ready!" I was so excited for two reasons: I was being a treasure seeker like Mr. Williams was asking us to be, and...

I would get help on my awful MATH!

Ding. I looked over and Eva had gotten another text. Again, she lost all color.

"Eva, what's going on? Is someone texting something mean to you?"

"It's okay."

"Do you care if I look at it? Do you know who it's from?"

"I'll just read it to you. But, I don't have any idea who it's from."

I gave her my full attention. I already had an idea of who would have sent it. I made a mental note to give Holly and Trent a piece of my mind later.

Eva then read:

YWN: *You think you are so pretty, and so much better than everyone else. Let me tell you, you're not. I think there are a lot of girls prettier than you, and beauty comes from the inside anyways. You may think you are all that, but you are dark and mean on the inside. -YWN*

"Who in the world would write that? And who is YWN?"

"My very first text said, *'your worst nightmare'*. But I don't know who it is, I have no clue."

"Did you do something to make someone mad?" I realized Holly and Trent let everyone know it was them, this person was using a secret name.

"No, I don't think so. I just go to school and come home. I don't even talk to people." Then she looked down at her lap. "I know people think I'm stuck up, but really I am just so shy. I get so nervous talking to other people."

"Gosh, I'm so sorry. Some people seem to love hurting other people. I just don't get it. How about we try to forget about this text and you come over today and we can have a good time."

"Okay, sounds good." And Eva's color was all back, and she was smiling.

Today was going to be fun, I couldn't wait for her to hang out with Grace and me.

As I walked off the bus I realized I forgot to ask her what phone number the text was sent from. I'd just have to ask her later, if I remembered to.

After I got home from school, I went into the kitchen to grab an afternoon snack.

"You're having *who* over?"

"Eva, you know, the girl on our bus."

"I know who you're talking about. But you *can't* be serious!"

"Grace, why are you being like this? Why can't I have her over? You know we are supposed to be treasure seekers."

"I know, I know. But, couldn't you have anyone else over. Anyone, besides her, *please*?"

"What the heck is wrong with you? I don't understand!"

"She's gorgeous!"

"I know, so?"

"So? Don't you see? If Jonah comes over to work on the treehouse, he'll take one look at her and fall in love!"

I couldn't hold it in, I completely lost it and burst out laughing.

"Cat! It's not funny! I'm serious!"

"I know you are, that's what makes it so funny."

"Hmph, some sister you are."

"Come on, we're supposed to be nice to others, and you better not be mean to her because she's pretty. I mean, the girl can't help it that she looks like a model."

"I know," Grace said as her shoulders slumped. "I'm sorry, he's just so darn cute."

"And," I added, "you're only eleven years old."

"True love can happen at a very young age."

Trying to hold back more laughter I responded, "Yes, but eleven is a very young age. Give it some time sis." I put my arm around her and guided her towards the kitchen, "Just wait until you're more like nineteen or something."

"You're right, but while I'm eleven I can dream, can't I?"

As a giggle started to escape my mouth, I responded, "Dream away, Sis."

"Wait!"

I pulled my arm away and asked, "What?"

"I don't know his last name!"

"So?"

"So? Are you serious? Do you know what his last name is? How can a girl dream without knowing that detail?"

"Um, I think Dad said 'London', why do you want to know?"

"No reason, thanks." And off she went towards the pantry, but not before I heard her say under her breath in a dreamy voice, "Grace Elizabeth London, it's got a nice ring to it."

Rolling my eyes, I still couldn't stop a smile from stretching across my face. As I went to join her for a snack, I realized something.

I knew my sister was a nice person, and I knew she would be nice to Eva when she came over, but I couldn't believe she would even question having Eva over. After all we've learned and heard about bullying and being kind to others.

It was now that I realized something. Grace was jealous. It had caused her to act and say things that weren't the nicest.

Jealousy was not good. No, it could cause others to be mean for no reason.

No reason at all. Jealousy was not only bad.

It was a poison.

CHAPTER 17

"She's here!" I yelled out to Grace.

"Okay, I just have to go to my room for a bit."

Looking back, I watched Grace head down the hall. Strange, usually she would always beat me to the door when company came by.

As I opened the door, I greeted, "Hey Eva, come on in! So glad you could come."

She looked to her left, "Um, that boy on the bus is heading this way too."

"Oh, that's Jonah." I leaned out the door and yelled, "Hi Jonah! You coming to work on the treehouse some more?"

"Yup," holding up his tools, he pointed to my backyard, "Just heading that way," then he raised his hand, "Hi Eva, nice seeing you again."

"You too," she replied shyly.

"Hey Jonah, I'll help you!" Grace yelled, barreling out of the house, as she almost knocked Eva and I over.

"Grace, be careful!" I yelled out.

With a raise of her hand but not even a glance our way, she yelled, "Sorry." And then she was gone.

I looked over at Eva and apologized, "Sorry about that. My sister is usually a very nice person, she's just gone crazy over Jonah."

Eva smiled and answered, "It's okay, I can see why, he's kinda cute."

"Yeah well, don't let her hear you say that. She'll think she has competition!"

We laughed and walked in to start our math homework.

After an hour I asked, "Do you want to go out and see the treehouse that my dad and Jonah are building for us?"

"Sure, would love too."

"Great! Let me just grab Jonah and Eva some hot chocolate and cookies. They probably want an afternoon snack."

"Sounds good. Have you had fun working on your tree house?"

"Yeah," I scrunch my face all weird like.

"What's that funny face for?" Eva asked.

"Oh, Jonah and my dad seem to get along so well. In fact," I chuckled, "he seems to get along with adults more than kids our own age."

Eva stared at me and added, "I completely understand. I do too."

"Well, I can be working out there with them, and they just talk and laugh the whole time. I actually have fun listening to them. They're kinda funny."

"Good," Eva said smiling, "then let's go see this tree house I keep hearing about."

So, we headed out and heard hammering coming from inside the treehouse.

"Hey, guys, how's it going up there?"

"Great!" Grace yelled down. Her head peeked out the side, but she lost her smile when she spotted Eva. "Oh, you're still here."

With my mouth hanging open, I looked from Grace to Eva. Grace had a scowl on her face, while Eva looked down at the ground. I matched Grace's scowl. Just then the hammering stopped, and Jonah peeked out.

"Hey guys, it's coming along good. Come on up and see what we've done."

After we climbed up, we looked all around.

"Wow, guys, this is so cool! I can't believe how big it's going to be!" Eva exclaimed.

As Eva and Jonah talked, I glanced at my sister. She stood there, in the corner with her arms crossed, with a scowl aimed right at Eva and Jonah. I tried to get her attention, to tell her to knock it off, but she wouldn't take her eyes off them.

I just stood there and watched my sweet sister, whom I loved, act mean to my new friend.

What in the world was wrong with her? Could jealousy really cause someone to act so mean?

CHAPTER 18

Between the school tower and our treehouse, I stayed busy helping Jonah for three weeks. Winter had set in and it was the beginning of December. It was cold, but we hadn't had much snow yet. That probably meant we would get hit hard in January. So, my dad and Jonah worked every weekend to get the tree house completed.

During the weekdays after school, a group of us would go into the auditorium and work backstage as we helped Jonah build the tower. It had come along really well. I learned so much that I thought I was actually doing an okay job helping him.

Eva continued to get text messages from *"Your worst nightmare"*. All of them were mean, and we couldn't figure out who was sending them and why. At first, I thought they were from Trent or Holly, but I could tell they weren't. How were we going to figure out who was sending them?

Well, another school day was over, and today we were going to help Jonah again with the tower. I couldn't wait.

Tyler hadn't been able to come help because he was still in basketball and had practice every day after school. But today his practice had been cancelled so we were all able to go.

As we entered the auditorium, I could see it was coming together great. We were almost ready to start painting it. I could hear the music in the background already. Grace and Dallas always liked to have some playing while we worked.

I walked over to the guys and asked, "Hi guys. Jonah, what do you need me to do today?"

With his face tilted down at his plans, he responded, "Um, I need to cut some more wood, then hammer some towards the top." With his eyes on the paper he asked, "Cat, can you help me cut some wood, and Tyler and Dallas can work on the tower?"

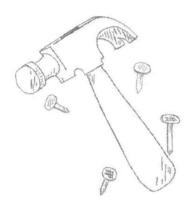

"Sure, I'd love too." Because I had been helping him for so long, I knew exactly what I needed to do.

"Great," and then he went on to tell the rest of the group what he wanted done.

"Come on Cat, let's go," Jonah said as he walked to the wood cutter.

I had been having so much fun doing this every day. "We have to wear goggles and hard hats, Mr. Dillion's orders." he said, as he handed me a hat and goggles. Mr. Dillion was our shop teacher and came every day to oversee the project.

I slipped my hard hat and goggles on and couldn't stop grinning.

He must have seen the goofy grin on my face because he paused and asked, "What's the silly face for?"

"I don't know. I just love doing this stuff!"

We walked over and found a straight piece of wood. Jonah started carrying it, when I looked over at the stage. There was music blaring and Grace, Becky, and Dallas were sitting on the floor looking at something, bopping to the music.

"What are they doing now?" I asked.

"They're picking out the paint colors.

They don't really like to work with wood and nails very much. They've gotten a few banged-up fingernails and decided painting may be more up their alley." He looked at me and asked, "Would you rather be picking out paint colors than cutting wood with me?"

I could tell he was truly concerned.

"Are you kidding me? I am having a blast. I don't want to sit around looking at colors when I can be cutting the wood, listening to the saw, and smelling the fresh-cut pine wood. I guess I'm just a tomboy at heart."

Jonah then nodded his head and smiled, "Okay, my tomboy friend, help me cut this piece of wood."

Turning a little red, I turned and grabbed the wood, "Okay, here it is. Now what size are you needing exactly?"

To my surprise Jonah didn't have me hold the wood while he cut, like he usually did. This time he let me cut the wood while he held it up.

As the machine turned off, I heard Tyler yell from up high, "You two almost done with that wood?"

"Yup, here you go." Jonah held up the piece of wood to Tyler, who was up in the tower.

"Guys!" I heard Becky holler, "Jonah said we could start painting the bottom of the tower tomorrow! I'm so excited."

"Yeah," Dallas added as she walked over to us, and handed Jonah a sample piece of paper that showed the paint color. "We picked out the color we like."

"Hey, I know! Eva is a fantastic painter. I can ask her if she would like to paint too!" I suggested.

"No!"

We all looked over at Grace.

"I mean," looking a little guilty, "I think we can all do it ourselves. If there were more people, we wouldn't have room to work around the thing."

"We'll have plenty of room. Cat, great idea, why don't you ask Eva to join us tomorrow." Jonah added, which caused Grace to twirl around and leave.

Everyone watched Grace leave, and they all turned to look at me, with a question in their eyes.

"What is wrong with her?" Tyler asked.

Shaking my head, I answered "I don't know. I have no idea."

CHAPTER 19

The next day school went by fast. It was time to work on the tower. We were so excited to start painting it. We couldn't believe how much we had gotten done in just three weeks. I was having a great time getting to know Jonah. Sometimes, I would forget he struggled with reading. I really didn't care anymore. The only time I even thought about it was when we were in class and kids would tease him.

Today was going to be extra exciting because Mrs. Hill said she would stop by and look at the tower. We couldn't wait to show her. We had asked her not to look at it until it was ready to paint.

We walked down to the auditorium, as everyone held different colors of paint cans, including a very shy Eva. In anticipation, we swung the cans as we walked.

Jonah opened the doors and held them open for all of us as we ran in, excited to work on the next phase.

"Oh no!" Becky exclaimed as she burst into tears.

"What?" I asked, as I came around the curtain. Oh my gosh, I could see what had upset Becky. We all just stood there, shocked. No one said a word, all we could hear were the sobs coming from Becky.

Where the tower had been standing yesterday, tall and strong, laid a pile of broken, smashed wood pieces. Someone or something had destroyed our tower.

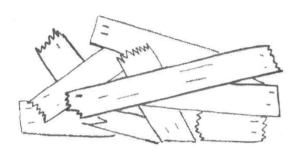

Just then we heard the door open and Mrs. Hill came in. "Guys, I can't wait to see what you have done. Mr. Dillion has told me so much about your tower. I feel like I can already imagine it."

Her words were cut off with a small gasp. We all stood there not knowing what to say or do.

"What happened kids?" My teacher asked.

"We don't know. Something must have happened. Maybe it wasn't built right. I'm not sure." I started to panic.

I watched as Jonah walked silently over to the wood pile, and Mr. Dillion came in and joined him. They both scrunched down and picked up pieces of broken wood.

"No, kids," Mr. Dillion said, "this wasn't an accident. Someone broke it on purpose."

****

On the bus ride home from school, I didn't feel like talking to anyone. Between the tower being broken and Eva getting those awful texts, I just wanted to hide in my room. Eva wasn't on the bus today, so I found a seat to myself and scrunched down to hide. What was going on? We had worked so hard on that tower. In fact, I don't ever remember working so hard on anything before in my life.

"Cat!" I heard my sister yell. I leaned over in my seat to see my sister headed my way, looking *not* too happy.

"Sit down when the bus is moving." The bus driver announced over the intercom.

"Grace, what are you doing?"

"Did you see?" She asked, as she pushed her phone into my face and scooted in next to me.

"See what?"

"This!" And before my eyes was a screen shot with a picture of me with hearts all around it.

"What the heck is that!" I yelled, as I sat up straighter.

"I don't know!"

"Well, who sent it?"

With a look of hurt, my sister answered, "That's the thing. I can't believe it!"

"What? What can't you believe?"

"It's from Jonah."

"What?" Was all I got out of my mouth before it was our turn to get off the bus.

As we walked off the bus, I tried to keep my head down as I walked with Grace and Jonah.

"Hey guys, are you okay if I come over and work on the treehouse a little more?" Jonah asked.

How could he act so normal? Did he really like me?

"Um, I don't know. We might be kinda busy today." Grace answered.

"Oh, okay." He turned to walk off, "Have a nice day."

Something did not make sense. There was no way Jonah would post something like that and act all normal.

"Hey, Jonah," I hollered as I tried to catch up.

"What?"

I held my phone up and asked, "Have you seen this?"

He looked at it and smiled, "Oh, Cat, it looks like you have a secret admirer. Who's the lucky guy?"

"You don't know?" I asked.

"No, but I can't wait for you to tell me. So, who is it?" He asked again.

I took a deep breath, squared my shoulders and looked straight at him.

"You."

CHAPTER 20

"What?" He grabbed my phone and looked at it closer. "But, I didn't make that! In fact, I don't even have an account!"

"Well, who would do that?" Grace demanded with hands on her hips. Then she added, "So you really don't like my sister?"

"What? No. I mean, no offense Cat, but we're friends, just friends."

I put my hand up to stop him, "I know, don't worry, friends on my end too."

"Whew," I heard Grace let out her breath.

"You know, I've heard of this stuff happening where people make fake accounts and then pretend to be someone else. It's sick." I responded.

"Yeah, I've heard there isn't always a way to find out who they are either. Sorry about that Cat."

"Good grief, you have nothing to be sorry for, I'm sorry someone did that to you. I wonder if it's the same person who is sending those awful texts to Eva."

"What texts?" Jonah asked.

"You know what? I think I need to get inside, I'm getting cold standing out here." And off ran Grace to the house.

I stayed out to explain to Jonah about the texts Eva had been getting.

"Man," Jonah said, "I just don't get why people have to be so mean. I agree Eva is pretty, but why would someone be mean to her because of that?"

A thought had just entered my mind. A thought that I didn't want to investigate, but I knew I had to.

"Um, I'm not sure Jonah, but I might have an idea." I turned and added, "You can work on the treehouse, see you in a little bit."

I rushed into the house and looked around for my sister. I heard her in the bathroom, so I looked around and froze. There sat Grace's phone, in plain sight on the kitchen table. I stood there and just stared at it. I had never been nosy and looked at other peoples' phones without their permission, but I knew I didn't have much time. Snatching it up off the table, I scrolled through her texts.

"What's this?" I mumbled. It looked like a new number.

I clicked on it and gasped.

"Hey that's my phone! Leave it alone!" Grace ran out of the bathroom and grabbed it from my hands.

I just stood there and stared at her, shock written all over my face.

I managed to whisper out, "Grace, how could you?"

She just looked at me and started to cry. I ran to her and hugged her.

"I'm so sorry, I didn't mean for it to go on this long."

Still in shock, I asked a second time, "But, how could you? Why?"

She sobbed into my shirt and answered, "I don't know! I don't know what happened to me. I'm such an awful person!"

I pulled back gently and guided her to the couch. "Tell me what's going on."

She sighed and grabbed a tissue off the coffee table. "I don't know. I just became this mean person. It came from inside me. I mean *deep* inside. I've never felt this way before towards someone. It started the day I saw Jonah for the first time. He was so cute! Then the first day we rode the bus, I was sitting with him, but he kept looking towards Eva. I thought he liked her."

"So? It doesn't make it okay to do what you did."

That made her cry again.

"I know! I thought if I made Eva feel bad, then maybe if Jonah talked to her, she wouldn't think she was good enough for him." She paused, "When in fact, she is a much better person than I am."

"Grace, you're a great person, I've just never seen you act like this before."

"I know! I haven't either. I used to get so mad at the bullies for acting so mean and sending such awful texts, then I became one myself."

"But why did you send such awful ones to Eva? She's *so* nice."

While she wiped away her tears, Grace finally was able to see and admit what had been bothering her for the past few weeks. "I'm so jealous of Eva." She slumped her shoulders and added, "I wish I was her."

"Oh Sis, I wouldn't want you to be anyone else but you."

"But I'm such a mean person."

I thought about it and answered, "No, you just let jealous feelings take over. I bet if you can let them go, you will be a great friend to Eva. The poor girl is so nice, but she is very shy. Everyone always says she's so stuck up, but really it's her shyness that keeps her from talking to others."

"I'm sorry Cat."

"I think you have someone else to apologize to."

Sighing and slumping her shoulders even more she whispered, "I know, you're right. I'll ride my bike over right now and talk to Eva." She turned, then walked off.

I yelled after her, "Hey, wait!"

She turned and looked at me with a question in her eyes. "What?"

"You didn't destroy the tower or make that fake account in Jonah's name by any chance, did you?"

"What?" Shock took over her face. "No way! I didn't do any of that, I have no idea who did."

"Hmm, okay, thanks. I didn't think you would have done that." Turning back around, I said to myself, "But I have an idea who did. Too bad I can't prove it."

CHAPTER 21

An hour later I sat on my bed doing homework when Grace walked in.

"Hey, how did it go?"

"Good," She came over and flopped on my bed, and held a bag in her hands. "I still feel so bad."

"What did she say when you told her?"

"She was shocked, but said it was okay." With confusion on her face she added, "But do you know what the craziest part was?"

"What?"

"She was shocked because she said she had no idea why I or anyone would ever be jealous of her. I looked at her as if she was crazy. Then the most amazing part came."

Now having my full attention, I sat with anticipation, "What happened?"

"She said she is actually jealous of me!"

"No way!"

"Yeah, she said she's jealous of all of us!"

Out of habit my hand instantly went to my forehead to feel my pimple. "Why in the world would she be jealous of us? That makes no sense."

"That's what I said. But she is jealous of us because we have so many friends and are so outgoing. She said she wishes she could be like that. Seeing us laughing and having a good time makes her want that too."

"I never thought about that before."

"I know," as she looked down at her lap my sister added, "and look at what she gave us for the treehouse." She pulled a painting out of the bag.

"Oh my gosh, that's beautiful!"

"I know, she said she was going to give it to you when the treehouse was done, but she was so excited she couldn't wait."

Studying the picture, I looked and saw it was a painting of our treehouse with a sunset, birds, and a lot of trees around it. It was amazing. I went and set it on my dresser and sat back down.

"She's so amazing, don't you think?" Grace acknowledged.

Smiling, I leaned over and gave my sister a hug, "I know she is, and so are you. Don't beat yourself up, just do what Mom says when we mess up. Learn from our mistakes, and don't do it again."

"You're right, there is no way I'm sending anyone mean texts again. And even though I think Jonah is *so* cute, I think I'll just be his friend right now." She placed her hand over her heart, and added, "Someday, down the road, maybe I will end up 'Mrs. Grace London'."

I threw my pillow at her and laughed, "Oh good grief!"

We ended up in a full-fledged pillow fight. The only problem was, my homework was in the middle of it all, and I would have to figure out what to tell my teacher tomorrow when I went to hand it in.

Right now, I was just so happy I had my sweet sister back. Sure, she was jealous, and man did it bring out the worst in her, but I was so glad she apologized. Now we could all be friends.

***

The next day in first hour, Mrs. Hill told us to keep our books in our bags because we were not going to do any work today. Everyone was so excited.

She had never said that to us before, so we didn't know what to expect. Instead, she said she was going to take us on a small field trip.

Wow, maybe my day would get a little better. I was still so brokenhearted about the tower. As we lined up, Holly asked, "Do we need to get our coats?"

"Nope, where we are going, you won't need them."

We all looked at each other. I looked over at Jonah and he just looked at his feet. He was still totally devastated from the tower being smashed.

As we walked down the hall, I noticed we were headed back towards the auditorium. Our teacher stopped us outside the doors and began to talk.

"Okay class, as you all know, about a month ago I asked Jonah to build us a tower for the school play and he and some of the kids here have worked after school very hard every day. I stopped by to look at it yesterday since it was completed and ready to paint." She then looked at each one of us and added, "Now, I want you all to see what I saw yesterday."

All of us who had worked on the tower stood at the back and waited until everyone else entered. As I started to walk in I turned and saw that Jonah hadn't moved. I placed my hand on his arm, "Come on, Jonah."

"I don't want to go in."

"Jonah, it's going to be okay."

We slowly walked in and stood towards the back of the group.

"Now, class. Tell me what you see." You could tell Mrs. Hill was not happy, she was saddened, but angry at the same time.

"A pile of junk," one student pointed out.

"Yea, how could they have worked on this for a month and this is all they have to show for it? I don't even build, and I could do better than this!" A girl mocked.

"I guess Holly was right. What did we expect from someone who can't even read the directions?"

They were all snickering and laughing.

"Stop," was all Mrs. Hill could get out. She actually had tears in her eyes.

"Listen to me kids. Is this really who you are deep down? Are your hearts this cold and mean that you can't see what I'm seeing? Jonah and these classmates of yours," pointing to us, "have worked non-stop every single day. They had a wonderful tall tower built, until..."

She looked again at everyone, until her eyes landed on Holly, then Trent. "Until someone destroyed it."

CHAPTER 22

Gasps went around the room. "Why would someone do that?" I heard a girl yell out.

"That's what I would like to know. Any thoughts?"

"Maybe someone doesn't like the play?"

"What?" A kid that was going to be in the play responded.

"There have been plays here forever and nothing has ever happened like this before. Any other thoughts?" My teacher asked.

Amy yelled out, "The new kid is kinda different. Everybody knows it!"

"Yea, but that doesn't mean we should destroy his work. He's worked hard on it." A boy said, looking down at the wood. "I saw Jonah working on this tower, he knew what he was doing. It was actually amazing!"

"Oh, come on, you've got to be kidding me." Trent said, "This just shows that he really is a loser. I mean, look at it, it's a pile of garbage." As he looked back at Jonah he finished, "just like him."

I was just about to open my mouth when Becky grabbed my arm and shook her head at me. I looked at her with a question in my eyes, but she pointed to the group and whispered, "Let them keep talking, I think some are sticking up for Jonah."

Sure enough, a new friend of ours, Tim, who had been playing basketball with us at lunch time, stood up for

Jonah. Even kids who had been laughing at him and teasing him the past few weeks were actually defending him.

"Hey, this is a sick thing to do to someone. It doesn't matter if they are different than us. He still did a cool thing here, something I could never have done." I heard one kid respond.

"Okay then class, what do you think we should do about it?" My teacher asked.

"Nothing! We sure don't want to help him. He's just a loser." Holly said in desperation. Looking around at the class she added, "Come on guys, remember who we're talking about. This is Jonah, the kid who can't read! Eighth grade and no reading or writing. Let's show him what this school does with kids who are different!" She pleaded.

"You know what, Holly?" A girl named Sue in my class said, "You are absolutely right. I don't know what I was thinking these past few weeks. I think we *should* show him what we do with kids who are different than us." She walked over and grabbed a piece of broken wood, walked it to the back of the group and showed it to Jonah. "What can I do to help?"

To my surprise, each student started to lean down and grab the broken pieces of wood, and walked them over to Jonah, each saying something kind.

"I'm sorry for how I've treated you, I'm willing to help you rebuild this."

"Sorry man, how can I help?"

"You're actually kinda cool. I'll help."

And so, on it went until there was a tall pile of wood at Jonah's feet.

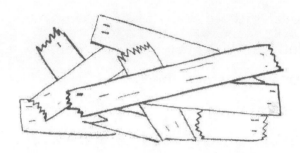

"Wait! You guys can't do this!" Holly stomped her foot. "He's weird! He's strange. He's so different."

"Yes, Holly," Mrs. Hill said, not hiding her smile which stretched from one eye to the other. "He is different," and she looked right at Holly, "and that's a good thing, a *very* good thing."

Mrs. Hill then walked over to Jonah, "Jonah, for the next few weeks, or however long it takes, we will all be coming here every day during the first hour and we will *ALL*," looking back at Holly and her friends, "be helping you build this tower back up, as high as it was before."

She turned towards the door and said, "Come on class. Oh, and remember, tomorrow wear grubby clothes as we will be cutting and hammering." And off she went as the bell rang to signal the end of class.

"Yea!" Dallas and Becky started hugging Jonah.

Laughing, I said, "Come on guys, give the guy some room, we have another class to get to."

And as we all started that way I heard Tim whisper to Jonah, "That was really cool man."

"Yeah, it was," was all Jonah could choke out.

CHAPTER 23

One week later we had the whole tower completed and ready to paint. I couldn't believe it! With all the help from the class, Jonah was able to rebuild it very quickly.

I was amazed at how all the kids who had been teasing him for the past few weeks were actually being nice to him. Some I could tell even looked up to him now. They were in awe of his building skills.

Eva had come to help paint today and Grace was right by her side, watching and trying to learn how to paint properly. I stood back and watched them because I couldn't believe the difference in Grace. Once she apologized, she was able to move on and become friends with Eva. With Eva's shy personality and Grace's not so shy personality, they were actually becoming great friends.

I watched as Eva showed Grace how to paint perfect strokes. Grace watched wide-eyed, but it never stopped her mouth from yapping a mile-a-minute. Eva just painted and giggled. A perfect friendship.

***

A week later the tower was finished just in time for the play. Eva and Grace had painted 'North Pole' across it and added lights. There was also a Christmas tree and a snowman way at the top. It looked fantastic!

And besides the cool tower, Jonah had also completed our treehouse. I was so excited to show it to everyone. My friends were all coming over to see it after school today. Tim had even said he would join us.

After we got off the bus, we headed into my house. We grabbed all the treats Grace had made. I announced, "Okay guys, are you ready to see our finished treehouse?"

"Yes!" They all hollered.

I looked over at Jonah, "Do you want to show them? Why don't you lead us out since you made the whole thing?"

"I didn't make the whole thing, I helped your dad," Jonah commented shyly.

"Come on Jonah," Tim started walking towards our back door, "show me this treehouse I keep hearing about."

And off we went with Grace, Dallas, and Becky running ahead of us to see it. All of a sudden, they stopped.

"What's wrong?" I asked.

But before they could answer I heard Tyler yell out, "Snow! It's snowing!"

Sure enough, I had been thinking so much about what everyone would think of the treehouse that I hadn't noticed the big, white, puffy flakes falling all around.

"Yay!" The girls yelled, twirling in circles.

"See if you can get any on your tongue!" Becky exclaimed with her head tilted up, arms outstretched, and tongue sticking out as far as it possibly could.

Grace hurried and laid her treats to the side and ran back to the group.

We all, with the exception of Tim, Jonah, and Eva, started to try to get snowflakes to fall on our tongues.

I peeked over to see Tim and Jonah both standing there with their arms folded over their chests, watching, and Eva had a shocked look on her face. I heard Eva ask the guys, "Are they always like this?"

"Pretty much," As they stood there watching us all twirl around, Grace and Dallas got so dizzy that they rammed into each other. Both fell to the ground, which caused bursts of laughter.

Tim answered Eva's question again, "Yup, this pretty much sums up this group." And that comment was followed by a smirk on Jonah's face and a bewildered look on Eva's.

"Come on, you two, I'll show you the treehouse." Looking around the group, Jonah smiled, "They may be awhile."

I noticed the guys and Eva climbing the ladder and I yelled out to everyone, "Come on, they're heading to the treehouse, let's go!"

And we all followed each other up the ladder.

"Oh wow! This is great!" Dallas's face glowed.

"It's so much bigger than your other one." With eyes roaming, Tyler tried to take it all in.

"It's so pretty. Oh my gosh! I love this picture! Where did you get it?"

Smiling I watched as the group huddled around the picture Eva had painted for me.

"Eva made it." I stated simply.

"What?" Dallas whipped around and looked straight at Eva.

"Yeah, Eva made it for the treehouse. Isn't it great?"

"Eva! I had no idea you could draw, or should I say, paint this well. I knew you could paint the tower at school, but this is amazing! It's actually fantastic!" Becky commented while she never took her eyes off the drawing.

That caused Eva to get totally embarrassed. Her face turned five shades redder than normal. "It's not that great guys, it's just a painting."

"Well, I think it's fabulous!" Dallas yelled out.

"Hey, I have an idea!" My sister exclaimed.

"What?"

"Well, Eva can draw, Jonah can build, I can bake, and we can all do different things than each other. It's like we all have different talents." She looked towards me and winked, "Well, most of us have talents."

CHAPTER 24

"What?" Scowling I just stared her down.

"Oh Grace, we just love Cat!" Becky leaned over to give me a hug.

"I know, I was just teasing her. But really, I don't mean talents, I just wanted to pick on my sis. There are eight of us in this treehouse and we are all so different from each other. I just had a thought."

"What is it?" Tyler asked.

"Well, when we have a birthday in our house, we have to all sit around and say one thing that we like about the birthday person. I just thought, what if we all sat and told something we like about the differences in each other."

"That's a great idea, Grace!" Becky exclaimed. But her face quickly went from excited to doubt.

"What's wrong?" I asked.

"Oh, nothing."

"Becky," Tim coaxed, "what's wrong?"

"Well," she twisted her sweatshirt ties, "um, it sounds like a great idea, but I just don't know if you guys will be able to think of anything special or good about me. I'm different from you guys cuz I'm so big." Looking down at the floor she added, "not much good in that."

"What? Don't you dare talk like that!" Dallas yelled out.

"Yeah," Grace walked over and linked her arm in Becky's, "we are starting with you. And look!" Pointing in the corner we could all see a toilet plunger, but the stick was stacked with toilet paper rolls. "Just in case."

Grinning, we all followed Grace to our new, second-hand striped rug that covered a good portion of the floor.

"Ok, let's start with Becky and say something we love about her." Grace started.

We all sat there, not knowing exactly what to say. To my amazement Tim spoke first.

"I do have to say, I know exactly what I like about Becky. It's her excitement. That first time you asked if I wanted to play basketball at recess, I kept looking over seeing Becky's arms flailing and cheering me on." He looked straight at her, and added, "I have never had anyone cheer for me about anything before that day. Thank you."

Grace was on her feet grabbing the toilet paper.

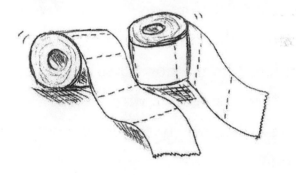

Handing Becky a roll, Becky took it and ripped off a strip, to wipe the tears falling into her lap.

"I want to say something." I said, raising my hand. Looking at Becky I added, "When I first started talking to you, I thought nothing could hurt you.

You always had a smile on your face. Now, the more I get to know you, the more I see the tears. Your eyes seem to be a constant sprinkler."

As people chuckled, I added, "I know you used to have a fake smile on your face all the time, now it's gone, and you cry all the time because you care so much. I don't know what changed."

It got quiet, I didn't know if anyone was going to say anything, but Becky added, "Thank you guys." Playing with her toilet paper roll, she added, "I can explain why I cry now and don't have that fake smile on my face. Before, the fake smile covered my heart that wanted to cry. But now, with you guys," she looked around the group, "I can finally be myself."

"I totally agree." Dallas piped in. "That is what is so wonderful about this group. We can all be ourselves. It doesn't matter that we are all a little different than each other, everyone accepts each other for who they are."

"I'll go next. I love Grace's food!" Patting his stomach, Tyler reached over in the middle of the circle and grabbed another brownie. "I can't wait to get here every time to see what she has cooked up."

"Yeah," Jonah also patted his stomach, "I think I've gained ten pounds since I moved in next to you."

To her own surprise, Grace opened her mouth and said, "But it looks good on you."

Her hands flew to her mouth and her eyes got huge. Mumbling behind her mouth she slurred, "Did I just say that out loud?"

CHAPTER 25

We all burst out laughing. Well, all but Grace and Jonah. Both their faces turned beet-red.

We all took turns talking about each person in the room. We laughed. We cried. But it was awesome. With Jonah the only one left, I had something I wanted to say.

"Okay, Jonah, you have taught me so much these past few weeks. When I first met you, I thought the best way to be a friend was to help teach you to read." Now, feeling foolish for having to admit it, I continued. "I'm sorry about that. I thought if I taught you to read then you wouldn't get teased. I wanted to fix you."

Taking a deep breath, I sat up as tall as I could, straightened my shoulders and looked right at him. "But there was just one problem with that. One big problem."

He looked at me with a question in his eyes.

I answered, "I wanted to fix you..." I paused and continued, "but you weren't broken."

"Oh!" Becky gasped and grabbed some toilet paper.

"There was nothing to fix. I thought because you were different, we needed to make you like us, but I was so wrong. Just because you're different, that doesn't mean it's a bad thing. It's actually a great thing. If you were like us, we would never have this amazing treehouse!"

"Yes!" Grace exclaimed as she threw her fist in the air.

"And we wouldn't have the cool tower for the school play! I bet that's what Mr. Williams meant by finding good in someone being different!" Dallas added.

Before Jonah could answer us, I felt myself being pulled into someone's arms. I tried to tilt my head, so I could see what was going on. We were in a big pile on the floor. The girls had tried to pull everyone into a group hug.

"Come on Tim and Jonah, come join us!" Grace hollered from the middle of the pile.

I looked and saw them standing to the side, looking a little lost as to what was going on.

Tim turned his head and looked out the window.

"Hey guys," He said trying to get our attention. "I hear something."

We all slowly got out of the huddle and looked over at Tim.

"What do you hear?" Tyler asked.

"I don't know, listen."

We all tried to listen for what he had heard.

Then I heard it. A faint voice, it sounded like someone was yelling.

"Look guys," Tim pointed out the window, "there's a kid down there in the grass looking up at us. I think he's yelling something."

As I looked out, my sister said, "Oh, that's Sammy, he's in my grade. I think he lives a few houses over."

We looked at her with a question in our eyes, but Grace answered it for us. "He's in the special-ed class, he's kinda different."

"Well, we know that different doesn't mean 'bad' now, does it? Let's see what he wants." Becky got up from the floor.

We went over to the open area where the ladder was. I laid on the floor to look down to see what Sammy wanted.

I cupped my hands around my mouth and yelled, "What?"

"C... can I... I play too?" he yelled up to us.

As I was just about to answer, my eyes connected to his, and I started to see stars...

Books by Paula Range

THE VISON SERIES

#1 - I AM "NOT" A BULLY

#2 – I AM A TREASURE SEEKER

#3 – I AM DIFFERENT

BONUS- CHRISTMAS WITH FRIENDS
For Christmas 2019

NOTE FROM THE AUTHOR

No one is exactly like you. You are unique.

Do not look at others who are different than you as a bad thing. Look for the good in them.

Others are different than you; but you are different than them.

See the beauty in being different. Life would be boring if we were all the same.

I tell kids to think of a rainbow. It would be quite boring if it was all one color. It is all the different colors that make it so beautiful.

To find when the next book will be released please visit me on Facebook at:

www.facebook.com/paularangeauthor

Feel free to leave a review on Amazon to tell me what you think about Cat and her friends!

I love to hear from my readers. Please feel free to write me at:

paularangeauthor@gmail.com

ABOUT THE AUTHOR

Paula Range lives in the Midwest with her husband, and five children. After being a stay at home mom for 18 years, she has started her love for writing children's books. She has also been subbing and loves talking with the kids about love and kindness.

Made in the USA
Columbia, SC
15 March 2020